SUGAR CANE

A CARIBBEAN RAPUNZEL

PATRICIA STORACE

PICTURES BY
RAÚL COLÓN

JUMP AT THE SUN

HYPERION BOOKS FOR CHILDREN
NEW YORK

First Edition

1 3 5 7 9 10 8 6 4 2

Reinforced binding

This book is set in Celestia Antiqua.

Printed in Singapore

Library of Congress Cataloging-in-Publication Data on file.

ISBN-13: 978-0-7868-0791-8

ISBN-10: 0-7868-0791-1

Visit www.hyperionbooksforchildren.com

For Martha Miller
and in memory of Henry Castel
Omnia mutantur, nihil interit —Ovid
—P.S.

For Guillermo Uria, who fixed broken hearts
—R.C.

COME, SIT on the balcony and look out over the sea. I have a story to tell you. It happens on an island where the waves follow each other, one after another, to the sandy shore. The waves are always beginning a story that never comes to an end. You can hear them when they touch the shore, saying

Once . . .

Once . . .

Once . . .

ONCE A YOUNG FISHERMAN and his wife lived together in a rainbow-colored house on the beach. They could see the sea when they opened their shutters at dawn, and the water glittered blue and green. During their afternoon nap, the sea sparkled through the clouds of netting that island people sleep under so mosquitoes won't bite them. When they sat on their balcony after supper at night, the water was dark as sleep before dreams rise. One sunset, when the husband and wife were swimming in the soft cradling waves, she told him they were going to have a baby. The fisherman was as happy as if he had unwrapped a present and found the very gift he wanted.

A few days later, the fisherman's wife begged him to bring her some fresh sugar cane. "Maybe this child will have a sweet temper," she said. "The baby will not let me rest without something sweet to eat."

Now, the sea is a good place to find fish and shells, but sugar cane will not grow in the sea. The fisherman did not want to make a long trip away from his wife to the center of the island, where he could find the sugar farms. He brought her a pineapple instead. "Pineapple is sweet," he said.

She answered, "This baby wants sugar cane."

He brought her star fruit and custard apples. "Star fruit and custard apples are sweet," he said.

She answered, "This baby wants sugar cane."

He brought her a ripe, delicious coconut. "Coconut meat and coconut milk are sweet," he said.

"Please," she said. "Please. This baby craves sugar cane."

The fisherman grumbled a little, but the next morning, he set out to find sugar cane for his wife. He walked and walked under the hot sun, but by midday he was still a long way from the farms where sugar cane grows. So the fisherman turned from the road and entered a thick forest to rest in the shade. He sat down under a tree and ate the lunch his wife had lovingly prepared for him. There

was spicy chicken, juicy mango, and tart ginger ale. Then he fell asleep.

When he awoke, the fisherman noticed a path he had not seen when he had first entered the forest. It led to a grand house built of pale coral and surrounded by a stone wall. Moving closer, the fisherman found a wrought-iron gate, disguised by its painted design of green vines and blue flowers. He pushed open the gate and found himself inside a garden. Every kind of plant, flower, and tree that grew on the island bloomed in the garden. And in one corner, near the door of the house, he spied a thick stand of sugar cane. The fisherman knocked on the door. There was no answer. He waited, but soon began to worry about his wife.

No one will miss the few canes I will take, he thought. He cut a few stalks and hurried home.

When the fisherman's wife saw her husband at the door, she could hardly wait to taste the sugar cane. Quickly she cut the cane into short sticks and put them in a bowl. Sweet syrup oozed from the cane, and she chewed as if she could never get enough. "Oh, thank you, thank you," she said to her husband. But even after all the cane was gone, her hunger for it stayed awake. The longing for sugar cane was moving inside her like the sea's waves surging outside.

She dreamed of the taste of sugar cane at night and thought about it during the day. Her husband saw she would have no peace without it, so he set off once again to find more sugar cane.

"If this baby is a girl," he said, laughing, "we are going to have to name her Sugar Cane. The name will show her how much we loved her even before she was born."

The fisherman walked the same hot road, and slept in the same dense forest. After his nap, he found his way to the same grand house. Again he knocked, but found no one home. Surely, here, he thought, where the ground was covered with flowers and the orchard above him studded with fruit, no one would grudge him a few stalks of sugar cane. He cut the cane, but when he was ready to start home, he couldn't find his way out of the sugar-cane patch. He turned around and around, but found himself trapped in a jail of sugar cane, locked in by the stalks. Behind him, he heard a sound, and turned to face a tall woman wearing a mask. Scaly lizards trailed around the skirt of her dress.

"Thief!" she shouted. "What are you doing in the garden of Madame Fate?"

The fisherman dropped the sugar cane and began to shiver, even under the hot sun. Everyone on the island knew the name of

Madame Fate. She was a famous sorceress. No one had ever seen her face—she always wore a mask, like the ones people wore at carnival time. People said she could make hurricanes. They said she traveled through the islands in dreams. They said she could make sharks dance in a circle and snakes pull wagons. They said she could put people to death and bring them back to life.

The fisherman began to explain. "My wife and I are going to have a baby. Sometimes, before they are born, babies will talk to their mothers and tell them how much they want a thing. Our baby wants sugar cane. And it does not grow where I live. I found it here. I am sorry I took it, but I will pay for what I have taken."

"You will pay for what you have taken," agreed Madame Fate. "You will pay a high price. You have taken sugar cane from me, and I will take Sugar Cane from you." The sorceress was so powerful that she already knew the baby's name, and she knew that it would be a girl.

"Not our child!" the fisherman pleaded.

Madame Fate bent down and picked a green plant. "You see this?" she asked. "With this I can make you forget who you are. Then you will be my zombie. You will work for me forever. Instead, you had better take your cane and go home. On the child's first birthday, I will come for her."

When the baby was born, the fisherman's joy almost made him forget Madame Fate. Sugar Cane was a beautiful, laughing child with skin as glowing and velvety as a black pansy. She loved to be taken for a dip in the waves, and she loved to hear her parents singing while they worked or sat with her. And just as her mother had predicted, she had a character like the taste of sugar cane—very strong and very sweet at the same time.

On the day of her first birthday, Sugar Cane's father took the baby and her mother to stay in a borrowed house sheltered in a cove far from where they lived. He wanted to try the fishing there, he told them. That night, they had a special birthday supper, and for dessert, a cake frosted with coconut. Sugar Cane's mother had made her a sea-coral necklace the color of sunset. She fastened it around the baby's neck, and they sang songs to her until they all were sleepy.

Toward dawn, the fisherman and his wife were shaken awake by a storm. Rain beat on the roof like animals running in flight from hunters.

By their bed stood a tall woman in a carnival mask. They heard her voice over the rain and thunder.

"Thief and cheat, you gave me pain.

Now you will pay with Sugar Cane!"

The masked woman reached under the cloud of netting, took the baby, and vanished into the night. Sugar Cane's parents searched for her for years, but no one had ever seen or heard of her. Sugar Cane's father returned again and again to the forest where he had first stumbled upon Madame Fate's garden, but the path had disappeared. Still, they never stopped searching.

Madame Fate took Sugar Cane all the way to a rocky coast on the other side of the island. There, the little girl grew up in a tower overlooking the sea, with only a pet green monkey named Callaloo for company. Madame Fate visited her often, and every day Sugar Cane grew more and more beautiful. Her thick gleaming hair curled like grapevines, and when Madame Fate returned from her travels, she would call from the foot of the locked tower:

"You live in a tower without a stair,

Sugar Cane, Sugar Cane, let down your hair."

And Sugar Cane would let down her hair like a ladder for Madame Fate to climb up.

The tower surrounded an inner courtyard garden, where there were tall trees to sit beneath, fountains where cool water danced, and one mosaic wall that

magically altered every day to show a new picture or the words of a poem. Sugar Cane loved the bright flowers and fruits of her garden. She loved the clouds of butterflies that flew into one of her tower bedroom windows and settled on the flowers she kept there. But she was sad when they flew out the opposite window that faced the sea, where she could not follow them.

Sugar Cane's foster mother saw to her education. Since Madame Fate was a conjure-woman who could bring people back from the dead, all Sugar Cane's teachers were special. An angel from the heavenly choir taught her to sing. Her guitar teacher was

a five-hundred-year-old Gypsy from Spain, and her piano teacher a jazz master from New Orleans. An Arabian philosopher tutored her in mathematics. She learned poetry from a Greek epic poet, and storytelling from an African griot. She learned cooking from the very woman who first invented ice cream.

Sugar Cane relished all her lessons and was fond of her spirit-teachers, but there was nothing she cherished more than music. She loved to play the piano while Callaloo turned the pages of her

music. But, with no other companion, she was lonely. Often at night, when the moon rose, Sugar Cane would stand at her window and sing. Her voice would float over the water, and her own words would return to her. The echo made her imagine another person answering her song. But she

always knew what the echo would say. Then the world would look as sad as she felt. The full moon would seem not like a shining other world, but like a tear, like the silvery drops she could see in her own eyes in the mirror.

One night, though, someone did hear her song.

Every year at carnival time, music contests were held on the island. For the past three years, a handsome young man, the son of a fisherman, had been named the King of Song. Now everyone called him "King." Often at night King would take his boat out. He would fish a little, dreaming of new songs, or drop anchor and try out tunes on his guitar.

One sweet-aired, still night, King steered his boat toward a bay he had never before explored, playing with the pieces of a new song. It was about a girl who lived in the ocean. Just at that moment, he looked down and saw that his oar was tangled in rippling black waves of hair that belonged to the most beautiful girl he had ever seen. Stars drifted across her shoulders and sparkled in her hair as she floated in the water.

It was the girl in his song come to life. Her face wavered in the water, maybe there, maybe not, like a dream deciding whether or not to come true.

Then King heard music. A girl's voice was singing the same words that began the song he had just been making up. He looked up and saw the strangest sight he had ever seen.

High above the water, in a stone tower, stood the girl he had seen

in the sea. Her hair looped around the tower all the way to the ground. As he watched, he saw a shadowy figure approach, and heard a chant:

"You live in a tower without a stair,

Sugar Cane, Sugar Cane, let down your hair."

The figure climbed up the vines of hair and disappeared into the tower. King stayed very quiet, not sure what to do next.

Some time later, King saw the girl framed again in the window, as her visitor departed in the same way she had arrived. King wanted to meet the girl as much as he wanted to finish a song he had begun. He wanted to meet her as much as he wanted to eat when he was hungry. He knew he had to try.

King moored his boat in a hidden cove and stepped onto shore. He walked around the tower, but there was only one way inside that he could see. He softly sang the chant he had overheard. Before he had finished, cascades of hair tumbled down the tower wall. Gently, he took hold of the thick curls and began to climb the flowing waves. It was like diving, except upward instead of down.

At last he reached the window where he had seen her. He rested his arms on the stone ledge and peered inside.

When Sugar Cane saw a stranger at the window, she was startled.

She had never seen another person, after all; only Madame Fate and her spirit-teachers. And never had she seen anyone so handsome.

The stranger's dark face glowed, lit by the full moon right above his head. She thought he must have dropped from heaven.

"Are you from the moon?" Sugar Cane asked.

"No," the stranger said, "I'm from this island. My name is King. Are you by any chance from the sea?"

"The sea?" she said, and laughed.

"I saw you in the sea, and heard you sing some of the song that was in my mind," King explained.

"I'm not from the sea," she said. "My name is Sugar Cane, and I live in this tower."

"Would you mind if I came in? My arms are getting a little tired." King waited until she nodded, then climbed all the way into the room. Once inside, King heard a creak. A bureau drawer in the corner of the room opened a crack, then snapped shut.

"Does your furniture usually move by itself?" he asked a little nervously.

"Oh, that's just Callaloo," Sugar Cane said. "He's my pet monkey. I guess you could say he's not brave. But the way I think of it, he knows everything about being a friend, and nothing about being an enemy. Come on out, Callaloo."

The top of a furry green head edged up from the drawer, followed by a pair of round, dark eyes. As soon as the eyes caught sight of King, the head ducked back down.

"It's all right, Callaloo," Sugar Cane said. "Come meet a new friend." Callaloo scrambled out of the drawer and jumped onto Sugar Cane's shoulder. "This is King," she said. Callaloo politely offered a green paw for King to shake.

"Does he like sweet things?" King asked.

Sugar Cane nodded. "You've never met anyone with a sweet tooth like his. Ice-cream cones, candied ginger, bananas baked in sugar . . . and he eats molasses with a spoon."

King had a slice of black cake—an island treat made with cherries and raisins and burnt-sugar syrup—in his pocket. He offered it to Callaloo. Changing his mind about their guest, the monkey sat on King's lap to eat the cake. Soon King and Sugar Cane were talking like old friends.

While Callaloo licked his paws, King looked around the room. "You have a guitar!" he said happily.

"Oh, yes," said Sugar Cane. "And a flute, and a piano, and a cello, and a harp, and some drums. I love music more than anything."

"I can play the guitar," he said. "I love to write songs. Shall I play you a song I wrote?"

"Yes, please," said Sugar Cane, and King began to play. First, he played the song from the contest that had made him King. Then Sugar Cane taught him a new song. Then King played another of his own songs, and Sugar Cane took up her flute. She scattered music into his tune like seeds into a garden. The song came to life in a different way when they played it together.

It seemed more real than where they were now or where they had ever been. Then the song changed its singers, and Sugar Cane and King, too, came to life in a different way. Callaloo danced on the top of the chest of drawers.

The music gave them another way of talking. King wanted to ask Sugar Cane why she lived by herself in a tower, but he felt shy. Sugar Cane wanted to tell him about Madame Fate, but she was afraid. With the chords of the guitar and the sound of the flute, the question and answer became part of the song.

Soon Sugar Cane noticed that the sky was changing color.

"It's almost morning," she told King. "You have to leave now, or we'll get in trouble."

"All right," King agreed, "but I promise I'll come back to see you in a few days."

He climbed Sugar Cane's hair back down the high tower, and when he reached the ground, he whistled the first eight notes of the song he had been thinking of when he saw her face in the sea. He heard an answering whistle. Then he hurried to his boat and sailed away.

Later that day, Sugar Cane's drawing teacher, who had painted murals thousands of years before in Egypt, noticed how tired she was. She was supposed to practice drawing birds, but she fell asleep

over her lesson. The spirit-teacher pulled her paper from under her head, and saw that it was covered with sketches of a young man's face. He smiled.

King was thinking about Sugar Cane as much as she was thinking of him. Only a few nights later he stood at the foot of the tower and whistled the first eight notes of their song. Sugar Cane let down her hair in reply. Again they stayed up talking and making music. King even remembered to bring some guava jelly for Callaloo.

Sugar Cane could not hear enough about the world that King lived in outside the tower.  There were streets and markets and families and parades, things she had never seen. And King was amazed by Sugar Cane's stories of her own life—both inside and out- side the tower. Even though she never left the tower, she had visited many worlds with her spirit-teachers, who taught lessons from other times and places.

Soon Sugar Cane heard King's song over the waves every few days. Then she would let down her hair. She began to weave a

ladder from the strands of her hair. Then she would be free. She would leave her tower for this new world.

Sugar Cane began to feel King was with her during her lessons, and King felt Sugar Cane sitting beside him in his boat and singing with him when he performed with his band of musicians. They began to be together even when they were apart, something that happens when people love each other.

One night, King surprised Sugar Cane with a gift. He walked to the dressing table where she sat, and very gently fastened a red butterfly made of jewels in her hair. Another time, as Sugar Cane was brushing her hair after King had said good night, she found in it a gold barrette. It was shaped like a wave, with diamond sea spray at its crest. After that night, King made a game of bringing her a jewel every time he visited. She would put the jewels on when he arrived and carefully put them away when he left. They would play music together, while her hair sparkled with jewels like stars in the dark blue water outside. On the nights she didn't see him, Sugar Cane worked on the ladder. Soon she would leave the tower herself, and she and King would be married. On those nights, she sometimes wore her jewels. They made her feel King was nearby.

Sugar Cane was able to keep King's visits a secret, but she could not hide the new joy their friendship gave her. Her spirit-teachers saw it and were happy for her, but Madame Fate saw it, too. And Madame Fate did not like it at all. She began to pay Sugar Cane surprise visits,

hoping to find the reason for her new mood. One night, Madame Fate stayed longer than usual after supper, and she nearly caught King. She thought she heard someone whistling, but Callaloo broke a plate and drowned out the noise. Then he scampered out of the tower to warn King to go home. King and Sugar Cane knew now to be extra careful.

The next night Madame Fate brought Sugar Cane a pretty new blue-and-gold dress. Sugar Cane tried on the dress and sat in front of the mirror while Madame Fate began to braid her hair. Suddenly Madame Fate held up something that glittered in the light—the jeweled butterfly that King had given Sugar Cane. It had slipped underneath her thick black ringlets.

"This is no gift of mine," said Madame Fate, holding the gem up to the candlelight. "But a gift to you belongs to me." She threw the ornament toward the tower window. Instead of crashing to the floor, its ruby wings began to flutter. It hovered for a moment near Sugar Cane, then darted out the window. Sugar Cane reached for it, but it was gone. Madame Fate tried to catch it, but it escaped her grasp.

"The butterfly that King gave me!" Sugar Cane cried out.

"And who," Madame Fate said icily, "is King?" At the sound of her voice, Callaloo scuttled under the bed.

"My true love," replied Sugar Cane clearly. "My friend, the one I will marry."

Madame Fate seized a pair of scissors that lay on the dressing table. Her eyes had a cutting gleam like the scissors' metal blades. She took the braids and waterfalls of Sugar Cane's hair, sheared

them off, and threw them out the window. "Then go to him, you ungrateful girl!" She hurled the scissors onto the floor, slammed the door to Sugar Cane's room, and locked it behind her. Sugar Cane heard Madame Fate's voice chanting spells. Then she heard the sound of the tower doors slamming, one by one.

Sugar Cane did not waste a moment. She thought only of being safe from Madame Fate's fury. She ran to the cupboard where she had hidden the ladder she was making. It was almost long enough. She dropped the ladder over the ledge.

"Come on, Callaloo," she whispered. "Hurry, before she comes back." She stepped onto the ladder, climbed down to the last step, and jumped the rest of the way. The monkey had not followed her. "Where are you, Callaloo?" she said. "Come on, sweet boy."

Callaloo scrambled headlong down the ladder and jumped into her arms, clinging tightly to her neck. His closed fists were full of something. She hoped he had brought some of the jewels that King had given her, but Sugar Cane did not stop to look. She picked up one of her fallen braids and put it in her pocket as a keepsake. Then she and Callaloo made their way to the water's edge. Now where could they go? She wished with all her power that she would see King's boat gliding toward them, but the sea was dark and empty.

Callaloo put his paws up to her face to show her what he had brought. "Oh, Callaloo, it's candy." He had snatched up two fistfuls of jewel-colored candies in bright wrappers— emerald-, pink-, purple-, red-, and topaz-colored—his idea of help. "Never mind," she said. "You tried. You have one, and I'll have one."

Sugar Cane reached into the mound of candy. Her fingers closed on something hard. Nestled among the candies was the golden wave-shaped barrette King had brought her, and the pink coral necklace she had worn as a baby. "Wonderful, Callaloo! Maybe you've saved us after all." She was too big for the necklace now, but it fit her wrist like a bracelet. She fastened it on for good luck.

The moment Sugar Cane locked the bracelet on her arm, a strong wind began to howl. The earth began to shake, and the tower began to sway. Stones fell from it and cracked like dishes on the ground. Callaloo buried his face in her neck. They heard shrill words sound, as if the wind had become the voice of Madame Fate:

"*In savage sun, and in wild rain, find shelter, thankless Sugar Cane!*"

The sea rose into a wave that roared toward them like a huge open tiger's mouth. Sugar Cane turned to run, but the water rushed forward as if it were hunting them. She held tightly to Callaloo as it sucked them in. Together they whirled and rocked and spun blindly. Just as Sugar Cane thought they would be dragged to the bottom of the ocean, they found themselves floating on something as soft as silk sheets. Sugar Cane and Callaloo were resting on top of a giant golden wave shimmering with diamonds. It was the golden barrette King had given her, now transformed into sparkling surf. They lay on the crest of the wave, which was higher than her old tower, bright as dawn within the storm. They traveled on the golden wave as easily as birds fly on air, until it gently set them down in the busy port that was the island's capital.

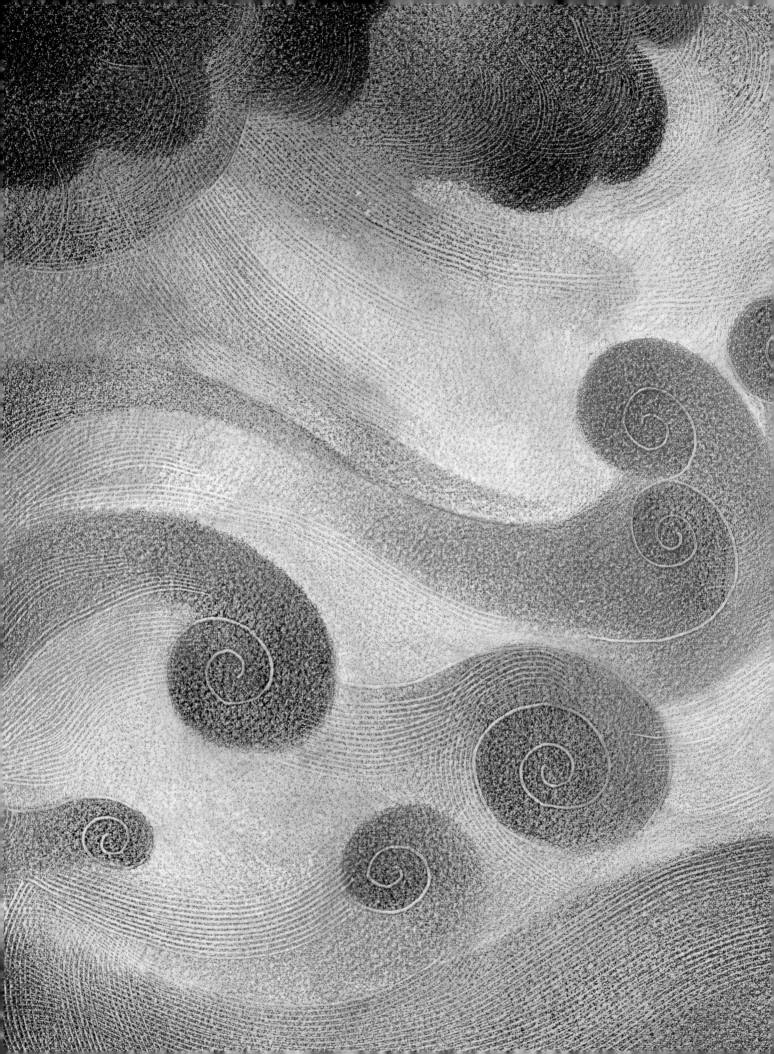

Sugar Cane was afraid and lost. She had never in her life seen a city. She held Callaloo in her arms and wandered past shops and statues and buildings. As she walked upward, amazed to be climbing the first hill of her life, some children who were playing in the garden of a fine house called to her. They wanted to play with Callaloo. The children gave Sugar Cane and Callaloo breakfast. When their mother came out, she offered Sugar Cane a place to stay in exchange for taking care of the

children and giving them lessons. So Sugar Cane and Callaloo were safe. They could begin to search for King among all these people.

King, too, was searching for them, though he could hardly believe he would find them. There was no trace left of the tower, or any sign that Sugar Cane had ever lived. He traveled to all the other islands nearby, hoping that Madame Fate might have hidden Sugar Cane elsewhere. But no one had seen or heard of Sugar Cane and Callaloo.

Months went by. Sugar Cane worked on making a guitar. When she carved and polished the wood, she felt as if she were talking to King. Finally, she fitted the guitar with strings she had woven from the braid she had saved of her hair. The guitar sounded sweet and strong and true. She would take the guitar to the great park high above the city, where she could see the mountains and the sea. She found a favorite corner there, near a pond where flamingos bathed and a waterfall raced down a cliff. She often took Callaloo and played music for hours. But she would never play the song that had been the secret sign between King and herself at the tower.

Sometimes she was too sad even to play other songs.

One afternoon, while Callaloo dozed, Sugar Cane sat quietly, holding the guitar in her lap, dreaming of King. Suddenly, a brilliant scarlet butterfly drifted onto the strings of her guitar. It walked up and down them, opening and closing its wings. With each wingbeat, it took another step, and with each step, it struck a note of music. They were the first notes of the song Sugar Cane and King had been singing when they met.

Sugar Cane looked up in surprise. Coming up the hill toward her was King. She was not sure he was real, but she held out her hand. When he reached her, he bent down and took the guitar

from her lap. Fastened tightly to the guitar strings, its ruby wings shimmering in the sunlight, was a jewel in the shape of a butterfly. Very gently, King unfastened the jewel and set it in Sugar Cane's hair.

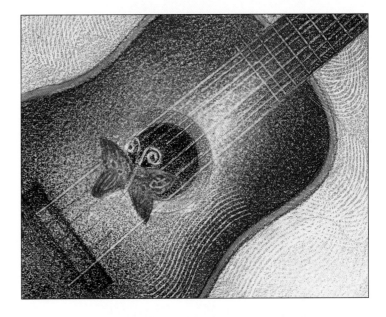

Then he took her hand.

Not long after that, King and Sugar Cane's wedding was held.

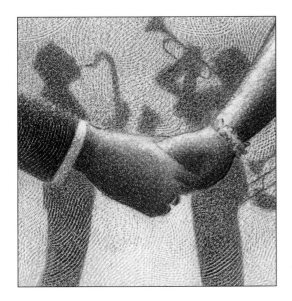

People from all over the town were invited, and a feast was prepared. There was even a second wedding cake, so Callaloo could satisfy his sweet tooth, for once.

Musicians from all over the island came to play at the wedding of Sugar Cane and the King of Song. People passing by were invited in to toast the bride and groom.

As the groom and bride joined hands for their first dance, someone in the crowd cried out. A woman had recognized the coral bracelet on Sugar Cane's wrist. It looked exactly like the necklace

she had made for her baby daughter's first birthday so long ago.

The musicians fell silent as the woman came forward with her husband. With their hearts pounding, the couple asked to see the bride's bracelet. On the back of the coral were the marks of Sugar Cane's initials along with their own. Their lost daughter was found at last. Sugar Cane's parents held her and her new husband in their arms, and wept with joy.

Then there was dancing such as this island had never seen. What did they dance? They danced the rumba, the bolero, the samba, and the mambo. They danced salsa and merengue and the limbo. They danced zouk, calpyso, sucu-sucu, and the cha-cha. Some of the people who went to that wedding are still dancing.

As for King and Sugar Cane, they loved each other more and more, and lived happily ever after. They lived so happily that they even remembered to wish love and happiness to you and to me.